Wilf

The MIGHTY WORRIER

BATTLES A PIRATE

D0806433

BATTLES A PIRATE

Georgia
Pritchett

Illustrated by
JAMIE LITTLER

Quercus

First published in Great Britain in 2015 by

Quercus Publishing Ltd
Carmelite House
50 Victoria Embankment
London EC4Y 0DZ

An Hachette UK company

Text copyright © Georgia Pritchett 2015
Illustrations copyright © Jamie Littler 2015

The moral right of Georgia Pritchett to be identified as
the author of this work and the moral right of Jamie Littler
to be identified as the illustrator of this work has been
asserted in accordance with the Copyright,
Designs and Patents Act, 1988.

All rights reserved. No part of this publication
may be reproduced or transmitted in any form
or by any means, electronic or mechanical,
including photocopy, recording, or any
information storage and retrieval system,
without permission in writing from the publisher.

A CIP catalogue record for this book is available
from the British Library

PB ISBN 978 1 84866 9 079
EBOOK 978 1 78429 2 652

This book is a work of fiction. Names, characters,
businesses, organizations, places and events are
either the product of the author's imagination
or used fictitiously. Any resemblance to
actual persons, living or dead, events or
locales is entirely coincidental.

10 9 8 7 6 5 4 3 2 1

Printed and bound in Great Britain by Clays Ltd, St Ives plc

For my boys

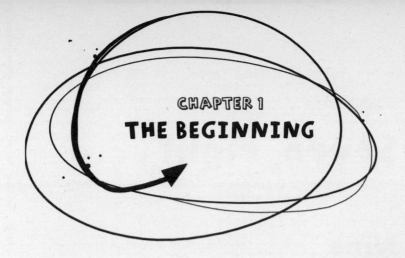

CHAPTER 1
THE BEGINNING

Oi!

What do you think you're doing? Close this book and put it back on the shelf right this minute. **Close it**, I said. Right, I'm going to count to ten.

One, two, three, four, five, six . . .

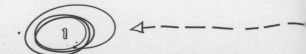

I mean it . . .

Seven, eight . . .

I'm not saying it again . . .

Nine . . .

All right, I'll say it one last time. Close the book . . .

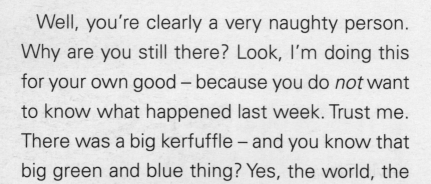

Well, you're clearly a very naughty person. Why are you still there? Look, I'm doing this for your own good – because you do *not* want to know what happened last week. Trust me. There was a big kerfuffle – and you know that big green and blue thing? Yes, the world, the great big old world – that almost ended. So, do as you're told and stop reading. I mean it. **STOP reading**.

Stop it!

All right, well don't say I didn't warn you. If you insist on reading what happened, don't come running to me when you find out it's a book full of sea monsters and pirates and people with big spiky poky things and the baddest, the baddest, the biddly boddly baddest most evil man in the whole wide world – Alan. And his right-hand man, Kevin Phillips.

So. You know that boy at school? Wilf. Yes you doooooo. Yes you do. The one with scruffly hair and pingy ears and a brain so full of ideas it's like a pan of popping popcorn. Well he only went and saved the world. **Again.**

Admittedly, Wilf isn't your typical superhero. He's not called Super-Wilf. He can't climb up buildings. And he's never been bitten by a spider THANK GOODNESS because Wilf is scared of spiders so if one actually *bit* him he wouldn't have time to turn into Spider-Man because he'd be too busy fainting.

In fact, Wilf is scared of lots of things:

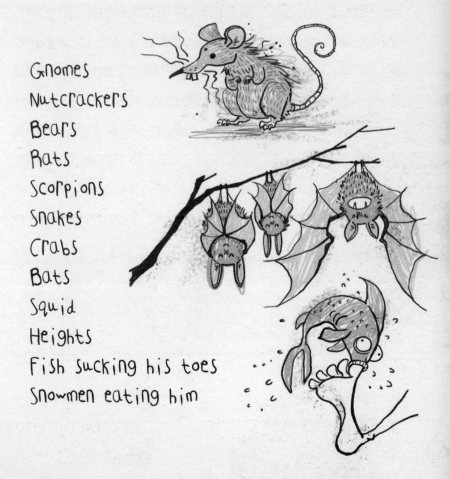

Gnomes
Nutcrackers
Bears
Rats
Scorpions
Snakes
Crabs
Bats
Squid
Heights
Fish sucking his toes
Snowmen eating him

Wilf has a little sister called Dot. What she lacks in size she makes up for in smells. She has a pig which has odd ears. When I say odd, I mean odd as in different to each other although, come to think of it, they are also odd as in odd. So the pig has odd odd ears. Some of you will know why Pig's ears are different – in which case, high five – and some of you won't – in which case, you've only got yourselves to blame.

Anyway, one ear is dirty and the other ear (and rest of Pig) is absolutely filthy. That's how you know which is the new ear.

Last week, Wilf received some post. It was a brand-new **'How to Stop Worrying'** leaflet. Wilf was so pleased when it arrived because he had been worrying that his **'How to Stop Worrying'** leaflet had got lost in the post, and then he would never be able to stop worrying about how to stop worrying. But here it was, all shiny and new and smelling of shiny newness.

He opened the envelope carefully, worrying that he might tear his **'How to Stop Worrying'** leaflet if he did it too quickly.

His mum walked past and saw him sniffing his new leaflet and said, 'You'll never stop worrying. You come from a long line of worriers. My father was a worrier, his father was a worrier and his father's father was a worrier. We've been worrying for generations.'

This gave Wilf an idea. He could look up his family tree and see all the worriers in history who he was related to. No sooner did he have the idea, he was straight on to the computer (stopping only to give the screen a good wipe, to hoover the crumbs from the keyboard and to disinfect the mouse).

Once he had printed out his findings, he took the family tree out into the garden to show Dot.

'Look, Dot,' he said, placing the paper carefully on the ground and holding it down with some stones. 'We are related to **Freddie the Fretful**. He invented the vest because he was worried people would catch chills.'

Dot picked up one of the stones and tried to fit it up her nose.

'And we are also related to **Annie the Anxious**,' said Wilf. 'She invented antibacterial hand gel because she was worried about germs.'

Dot popped one of the stones into her nappy.

'And our great-great-great-grandfather, **Norman the Neurotic**, made the very first "Mind the Step" sign because he was worried people might trip as they went into his house,' said Wilf.

Dot pulled one of her socks off and wiped her nose with it.

'And going even further back,' continued Wilf, 'there is evidence to suggest that we are related to the caveman who lived next door to the caveman who invented the wheel. Our ancestor invented the brakes,' explained Wilf proudly. 'What do you think of that?'

FREDDIE THE FRETFUL

WILF (THE MIGHTY WORRIER)

ANNIE THE ANXIOUS

NORMAN THE NEUROTIC

STONEAGE ANCESTOR

Dot chewed thoughtfully on the corner of the page, then scrumpled the whole thing up into a ball and threw it over her shoulder.

The ball of scrumple landed in Alan's garden. And THAT was when the

whole kerfuffle

started.

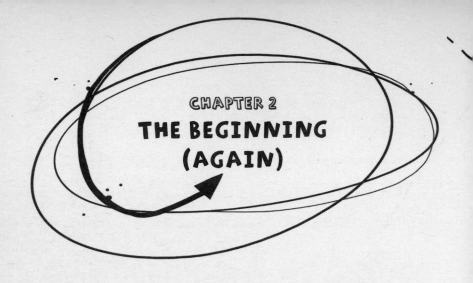

CHAPTER 2
THE BEGINNING (AGAIN)

'There's a ball of scrumple on my lawn!!!' screeched Alan. 'Somebody doooo something!'

Kevin Phillips tilted his head on one side and studied the ball of scrumple. He said nothing.

'Pick up that ball of scrumple!' commanded Alan.

Kevin Phillips turned and stalked off as though he had far more important things to think about.

'You are meant to be my right-hand man
and that means doing things like picking up
balls of scrumple!' shouted Alan after Kevin
Phillips.

Alan sighed.

He went and picked up the ball of scrumple
and took it into his house to show his wife
Pam.

'Pam, look at this,' said Alan.

Pam was watching reality TV.

'Look, it seems to be some kind of family tree,' said Alan, unscrumpling the paper.

Pam didn't respond.

'I wonder what *my* family tree is,' wondered Alan.

'Shh. I'm watching reality TV,' said Pam.

'Well can you stop watching reality TV and watch some reality instead?' asked Alan.

Pam sighed and turned to look at Alan.

'I think I'm going to look up my family tree,' said Alan.

'Yeah, there's a show where celebrities do that,' said Pam.

'Yes but I'm going to do it. For me,' said Alan.

Pam got out her phone. 'What's the phone number?'

'What phone number?' asked Alan, confused.

'Where I can vote you off?' asked Pam.

'Vote me off? You can't vote me off. I'm here.

I live here. You can't just vote me off!' he said and stomped down the stairs to his evil lair.

Alan spent the next few hours looking up his family tree.

Alan discovered that he had come from a long line of very evil people.

His great-great-grandfather had invented dentistry and had caused untold misery to countless people around the world.

His great-great-great-grandfather had invented school and ruined the childhoods of every child who had ever lived.

His great-great-great-great-grandfather had invented broccoli and had ruined the school dinners of all those children who had to go to school.

And his great-great-great-great-great-grandfather was Long John Alan, the fiercest pirate on the seas. He was feared by everyone who'd met him. And by people who hadn't met him but had heard of him. And even by some people who hadn't even heard of him.

Alan sighed. He wished he could be like Long John Alan and be feared and respected. All he had managed to do was scorch some eyebrows and spend all his money on a

Big Gun Thingy

with which he had failed to destroy the world **(see Wilf the Mighty Worrier Saves the World)**. Alan marched out into the garden.

'Kevin!' he called. 'Kevin?' he shouted more loudly.

'Where's my right-hand man?' asked Alan.

'He saw a squirrel and he went running off,' said Wilf who was pushing Dot on her swing.

'Doggy woggy,' agreed Dot.

'Shh!' said Wilf. 'Kevin Phillips doesn't know he's a dog. He thinks he's one of the family.'

'Doggy woggy woof woof,' said Dot.

'Shh,' said Wilf.

'DOGGY WOGGY WOOF WOOF!' said Dot, much louder.

'Dot, I want you to stop that,' said Wilf firmly.

'DOGGY WOGGY WOOF WOOF,' replied Dot.

'If you see Kevin,' said Alan, attempting to ignore Dot, which was not an easy thing to do because . . .

'DOGGY WOGGY WOOF WOOF.'

She kept shouting
**'DOGGY WOGGY
WOOF WOOF'** every
time he opened his
mouth to **'DOGGY
WOGGY WOOF
WOOF'** say
anything.

'Could you tell him I
need him,' said Alan . . .

'DOGGY WOGGY WOOF WOOF.'

'. . . because I have a plan.'

'Is it a lovely plan – to skip round the garden
or pick some flowers or toast a marshmallow?'
asked Wilf hopefully.

'No. It is an evil plan,' said Alan.

'Yes I thought you might say that,' said Wilf
sadly.

'I am going to be a pirate. Not just any pirate but the most fearsome pirate in the world.'

'But don't you need a boat to be a pirate?' asked Wilf. 'And a parrot? And an eyepatch?'

'Yes, yes, I know that,' said Alan crossly. 'But just say it again so that I can write it down.'

'A boat and a parrot and an eyepatch,' repeated Wilf.

'Yes, *obviously*,' said Alan. 'And I'm getting all of those things tomorrow. And then I will be the baddest, the baddest, the biddly boddly baddest pirate in the whole wide worlderoony.'

And that is when the

whole kerfuffle

started.

'DOGGY WOGGY WOOF WOOF.'

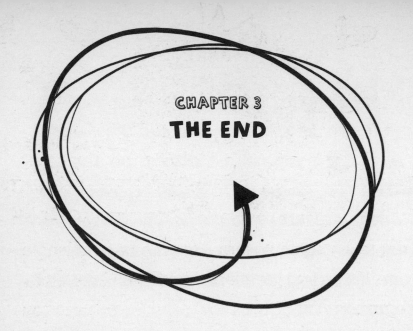

CHAPTER 3
THE END

The next day was – oh I don't know, it's exhausting describing things. You decide. Sunny? Rainy? Whatever you think. I wasn't really paying attention.

Luckily someone *was* paying attention. It was Wilf. Wilf was giving Stuart a run in the garden. Stuart is Wilf's pet woodlouse. But he is also his best friend. And the person Wilf tells all his secrets to. Wilf loves Stuart – all

TEN MILLIMETRES

SHINY SEGMENTS

FOURTEEN LEG

ten millimetres of him. He loves every single one of his fourteen legs. And each little shiny segment. And Stuart loves Wilf, from the top of his scruffly hair, past his pingy ears, past his knocky knees right down to his tickly toes.

The other reason Wilf was in the garden was because he was worried. Well, there's nothing new about that, but this worry was an **EXTRA BIG** worry about what Alan had said about the whole pirate thingy. He had tried knitting the worry away, but it hadn't worked. He had tried whistling a very long and complicated tune, but the worry was still there when he had finished. So he had come out into the garden to try to keep an eye on Alan.

Wilf and Stuart were practising hopping and while they were practising they were trying to look over the fence.

Stuart is tiny so he could see nothing at all, but if Wilf did a great big hop he could just about see between hops . . .

that something

Hop

Something big

Hop

had arrived

Hop

in Alan's garden.

Hop

It was a huge

Hop
wooden crate

Hop
with the words

Hop
'This way up',

Hop
on it

Hop
and a picture of

Hop
a pirate ship.

Oh no. Wilf was staggerblasted. He felt all shivery and blurry. His neck went all hot. And his knees felt like they might bend the wrong way. What was he going to do? He wanted to roll up into a ball like Stuart and he wanted to knit himself a big woolly hat that went over his eyes so he couldn't see what happened next.

But he didn't do any of those things. He had a great big old worry and then he had a great big old think and then he thought so hard that his brain needed a lie-down.

And then he had an idea.

Firstly, he would change his pants. If this wasn't a time for lucky green pants then he didn't know what was. Then he would go next door and try to find a way of stopping Alan from building his pirate ship. The only problem was that in between hops Wilf had noticed that Alan had also bought himself a garden gnome. Wilf was scared of gnomes. He was worried that they would come to life and bite his kneecaps.

Wilf went up to his bedroom and got out his shoebox of precious private things. Inside was his brand-new **'How to Stop Worrying'** leaflet. It had ten suggestions of things to do that might help. Wilf looked at NUMBER ONE.

1. Draw a picture of the thing you are worried about.

Wilf drew a picture of the gnome.

2. Think of the worst-case scenario.

Wilf tried to think about what would be worse than having his kneecaps bitten by a gnome. Maybe if the gnome was holding a nutcracker and cracking nuts. Wilf was scared of nutcrackers and hated the sound of cracking nuts because it made his eyes feel all scrunchy and his teeth feel all zzzzzzzzzzzzzzzingy in a scratchy way.

3. Make affirmations.

That meant saying positive things about yourself out loud to the mirror. The leaflet had some examples. Wilf tried one of these.

'I am a beautiful independent woman and I deserve to be loved,' he said. That didn't seem right. He looked for another one.

'I am a mature and successful man and my life is a miraculous adventure.'

That didn't sound right either.

Wilf felt depressed. He wasn't a beautiful woman, he wasn't a successful man, he was a small boy who was about to have his kneecaps bitten off. And he had to do something about it right now otherwise he would never grow up to be a beautiful woman or a successful man or *anything*.

Wilf got his backpack and he packed some knee pads to protect his knees, a magnet to attract the nutcracker and a big plastic bag to put the gnome in. Then he kissed Stuart and Dot goodbye and he climbed over the garden fence.

Wilf plopped down into Alan's garden and ducked behind a duck. An ornamental duck,

you understand, not
a real one. And then
he had a peep. A real
peep, not an ornamental
one. He eyed the gnome.
The gnome eyed him back.

Meanwhile, Alan had opened the big crate
and was standing studying the instructions
and scratching his head.

'Put plank A into slot B,'
said Alan.

Kevin Phillips scratched
his ear and then tentatively
sniffed his paw.

'This is the kind
of job I need a
robot for,'
said Alan.

He went to the door of his house and shouted, 'Mark III? Mark III? Mark III?'

No response.

Alan then used Mark III's full name, to show he was getting cross.

'LRX2FL309version8.4markIII!'

A few moments later, a tall gangly robot galumphed down the stairs.

'What?' he said bad-temperedly.

'I need some help,' explained Alan.

'I'm busy,' said Mark III.

'Doing what?' asked Alan.

'Playing a computer game. And don't tell me to stop because I've only been playing for five hours and I've almost beaten my high score.'

'The whole point of having a robot,' said Alan, 'is so that things will get done quickly, efficiently and silently.'

'Yeah, well, I didn't ask to be invented!' said Mark III and he stomped off towards the house, accidentally tripping over the gnome.

The gnome smashed into a hundred tiny pieces.

'My gnome!' screeched Alan.

'Sorry,' said Mark III, and he stomped back up the stairs to his bedroom.

Wilf did a little silent jig of joy. The gnome was gone. That silly bearded ceramic fool was history! Wilf's kneecaps were safe! And he hadn't even had to do anything! The robot had done it for him. So now all he had to do was think of a way of stopping Alan building his pirate ship.

Kevin Phillips sighed and gave Alan a look.

'I know, I know,' said Alan, 'he's going through a difficult phase. One day he'll come out of it. Perhaps I just need to make a few adjustments.'

Kevin Phillips sneezed in a disdainful way.

'Right, just you and me then,' said Alan. 'Plank A, plank A – right we don't have a plank A but we have two plank Cs so maybe if I stuff one of those into slot B. It doesn't fit. Right.'

Alan tried to pace up and down to help himself think, but Kevin Phillips was lolloping about and running round and round Alan's feet and tripping him over.

Suddenly Wilf had another idea. He didn't need the bag and the magnet for that evil nutcracking gnome any more. He could use them for something else. He put his knee pads on and, while Alan and Kevin Phillips were distracted, he crawled into the crate. He waited for a moment, as silent as an orange. Then he carefully got his magnet out and he held it up so that all the little bolts and nuts and screws for building the ship went pinging on to the magnet.

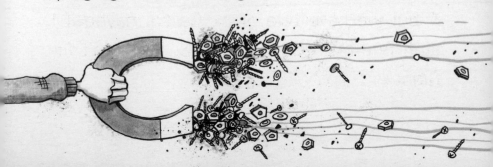

Then Wilf scooped them into his plastic bag. He worked as quickly and quietly as he could, listening to the muffled voices of Alan and Kevin Phillips outside.

'Right, Kevin,' said Alan, 'here's the hammer – you hold that for a minute.'

Kevin started busily digging a hole in the ground. Then he plopped the hammer into the hole and began to bury it.

'No, Kevin! No! Don't do that. Listen, I know I promised you I'd do something about cats . . .'

Kevin Phillips stopped digging and blinked at him from above his large muddy beard.

'And I promise after I've made myself a pirate ship, I will. In fact, I had a really evil idea – do you want to hear it?'

Kevin Phillips wagged his tail.

'You know how you want all the cats in the world to be wiped out by a meteor – just like the dinosaurs were? Well we are going to build ourselves our very own meteor, OK? How about that?'

Kevin Phillips bounded over to Alan and licked his ear excitedly.

'Yes, you like that, don't you?'

Kevin rolled over and Alan tickled the bit on his leg that made Kevin's back leg go all pointy.

'**Because I'm the baddest, the baddest, the biddly boddly baddest in the whole wide worlderoony,**' said Alan. '**And you are my werry special wight-hand man, yes ooo are, yes ooo are, yes ooo are.**'

And Kevin sat up and nuzzled Alan and Alan tickled the bit behind Kevin's ear that made his paw stamp.

'Right, dig up the hammer and let's get building,' said Alan.

Kevin Phillips yawned, circled once to the right, twice to the left, once more to the right and then lay down and closed his eyes and fell asleep.

'Right. Just me then,' said Alan sadly. 'Plank C into slot D and fasten with nut F . . .'

But nut F wasn't there. And neither was nut A, B, C, D, E nor any of the bolts and screws because they were all in Wilf's backpack and Wilf was scrambling back over the fence and into the open arms of Stuart (all fourteen) and the sticky arms of Dot.

Wilf had stopped Alan from making his pirate ship! Yay! So maybe Alan would give up and find something else he wanted to do. Something nice. Like Irish dancing. And maybe this is the end of the book.

THE END?

Let's peek over the page . . .

Of course it's not the end of the book, you blithering idiots! As far as Alan becoming a pirate – this is when the whole kerfuffle *started*. No but it really *is* this time.

Yes, Wilf had put a spanner in the works. Or to be more accurate, he'd taken a spanner *out* of the works because that had also pinged on to his magnet. But Alan wasn't going to let a little thing like that stop him. He was determined to become a pirate.

So once he had left some very negative feedback on the website of the seller of the pirate ship, and once he had ordered himself lots of tiny nuts and bolts and screws,

he got right back to making his pirate ship.
And a mere seventeen days later . . .

it was
finished!

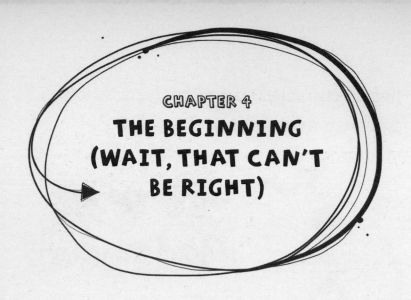

CHAPTER 4
THE BEGINNING (WAIT, THAT CAN'T BE RIGHT)

It was a beautiful day, pouring with sunshine. Or was it raining? Maybe it was cloudy. Some manner of weather was happening. You choose. I'm all out of adjectives.

Anyway, Wilf, Dot and Stuart were having breakfast.

Dot was face down in a bowl of crispies, sucking them up. Stuart was nibbling on one of the many crispies that had spilled out of

her bowl and Wilf was
dipping a toast soldier
in his egg.

'Dot, Mum is working today so she has
asked me to take you to the seaside,' said
Wilf.

'Tractor,' replied Dot.

Stuart did a little excited dance.

'Stuart,' Wilf said, 'I'm afraid you can't come to the seaside. Not after what happened last time.' And  he gave Stuart a stern sort of look. And Stuart blushed a bit. And tried to look like he was very interested in a crumb that was near him.

Wilf made a packed lunch for him and Dot. He was just packing it away in his favourite Tupperware when he noticed something hiding behind a Hula Hoop. It was Stuart.

'Stuart! I can see you! I told you, you can't come this time. You can come next time,' said Wilf.

Stuart was not happy. He rolled up into a ball.

'Stuart. Listen to me,' said Wilf.

But Stuart would not listen. Woodlice, as I'm sure you know, are terrible sulkers.

'Stuart!' said Wilf sternly. 'Unroll this instant.'

Stuart rolled up tighter.

Wilf sighed.

Stuart was going through a naughty phase at the moment. Wilf blamed himself. He had spoilt him. He would have to have a serious talk with him when he got home.

Wilf and Dot had to take two buses to get to the seaside, but Wilf had memorized all the bus routes and all the bus timetables so it was really very easy. Wilf liked maps and timetables because they are neat and orderly and everything is where it is meant to be and when it is meant to be, and that is very reassuring.

The bus ride is Wilf's favourite part of going to the seaside. Wilf doesn't really like the seaside because there is sand, and sand is very inconvenient. Dot, on the other hand, loves the seaside. She likes to dig and to throw sand around and to dip her ice cream in the sand and then eat it in an alarmingly crunchy way. Today, after only ten minutes, the combination of snot and ice cream and sand meant Dot was like a tiny pebble-dashed person.

Wilf watched all this patiently, a wet wipe in each hand.

As Wilf was watching, someone strode past, picked up Dot's bucket and spade and said, 'I'll be needing this for digging up all my treasure,' and then he marched off.

'My bucket and spade!' wailed Dot. Although when you're wailing, consonants go out of the window so it sounded more like:

'My rurret and raaaaaaaaaade!'

Wilf trotted after the person. But it wasn't just any old person – it was Alan!

'Excuse me, Mr Alan . . .' said Wilf. 'Could we have our bucket and spade back?'

'My name's not Alan,' said Alan. 'My name's Bluebeard.'

'But you haven't got a beard,' said Wilf.

'Fine, then I shall call myself Captain Scarface,' said Alan.

'But you haven't got a scar,' said Wilf.

'Fine, then I shall call myself Captain Hook,' said Alan.

'You haven't actually got a hook,' said Wilf quietly.

'Do you mind,' said Alan, 'I'm a little bit busy being feared and respected.'

'Yes of course,' said Wilf, 'but you took my sister's bucket and spade and it's her very favourite thing because it's red and it's good for digging and hammering, and digging and hammering are her main things, so if you could just give it back . . .'

'Does that sound like the kind of thing a pirate would do?' asked Alan.

'Yes,' said Wilf. 'A nice pirate.'

'Well I'm not a nice pirate. I'm the biddly

boddly baddest pirate in the whole wide worlderoony.'

'But where is your pirate ship?' asked Wilf, baffled.

'Right there. Tied up to the end of the pier. *The Jolly Alan*,' said Alan proudly.

Wilf looked over to where Alan was pointing – and there it was, with a big flag on the top with a picture of Alan on it.

'But you didn't have any nuts or bolts or screws!' stammered Wilf.

'No I did not. And I will not be purchasing another pirate ship from that particular seller, let me tell you,' said Alan. 'But I managed to buy some other nuts and bolts and screws and now I am going off to be a fierce pirate. So if you'll excuse me.'

And with that he stomped up the gangplank of his pirate ship, still holding Dot's bucket and spade.

Wilf tried to explain to Dot but she wouldn't listen. He promised her sweets and lollies and countless other buckets and spades – but nothing could console her. She cried and cried until there were two clean little paths where the tears had run through the sticky dirt all over her face.

Wilf realized he was going to have to go and get Dot's bucket and spade back. And *that* was when the

whole kerfuffle

started. (No but it **REALLY** was this time.)

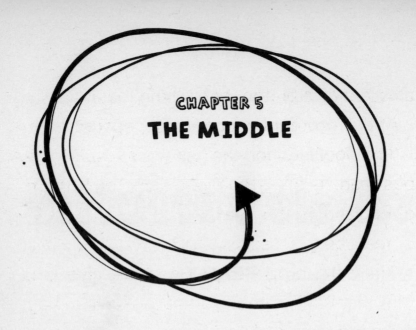

CHAPTER 5
THE MIDDLE

Wilf and Dot tiptoed up the gangplank, both holding their breath all the way. When they got to the top, Wilf saw Alan looking out through his telescope. Next to him was Kevin Phillips. Kevin was wearing a cone round his neck because he kept biting his bottom. And now he had a sore little bald patch on his big furry bottom.

Wilf scooped Dot up and went and stood,

as silent as a button, behind the mast.

At that moment, a postman appeared.

'I'm looking for an address,' said the postman. 'Is this – Big Pirate Ship, The Bottom of England, In the Sea?'

'Yes! Yes it is!' said Alan.

'I have a package for you,' said the postman. 'But there aren't enough stamps on it so you will need to pay 18p.'

'Damn!' said Alan. 'I've only been a pirate one minute and already I'm 18p down.'

While Alan was distracted, Wilf and Dot sneaked down the ladder and into the ship.

There were lots of cannons and barrels, but no sign of the bucket. There were hammocks and muskets and cutlasses and rats – eeeurgh, rats – but no bucket. There were big pirates and small pirates and pirates with wooden legs and pirates with beards and pirates with wooden beards, but no bucket. There were swords and knives and daggers and spiky ouchy things, but no buckets.

Suddenly Alan came running down the stairs. Wilf and Dot hid behind a barrel.

'Look, my parrot has arrived!' said Alan to Kevin Phillips excitedly. 'I ordered it online. I am going to call him Nigel.'

Alan brushed aside the packaging squiggles and was distracted briefly by the urgent need to pop a few bubbles of the bubble wrap.

'Watch this!' Alan said to Kevin Phillips.

'Pretty Polly, pretty Polly,' said Alan to the parrot.

Nigel blinked at Alan.

'Parrots can talk,' explained Alan to Kevin Phillips. And then he worried that Kevin Phillips would feel bad about the fact that he couldn't talk, so he quickly added, 'I mean, that's not why I got him – I just thought I *should* have one. If I'm going to be a pirate.'

Kevin scooted along the ground on his bottom.

'Look, watch. He will repeat everything I say,' said Alan proudly. **'Pretty Polly, pretty Polly.'**

Nigel stared back at him.

'Maybe they sent me a faulty one.'

Alan turned Nigel over and looked to see if there was somewhere he was meant to put batteries.

'Aaaark,' said Nigel in a discombobulated sort of way.

'Ah! You do talk!' said Alan. 'Right. Say pretty Polly.'

'Why would I do that?' asked Nigel.

'Because I said it,' explained Alan.

'So why would I say the same thing?' asked Nigel.

'Because you're a parrot. You parrot. It's in the name,' said Alan, a little impatiently.

'If you insist,' said Nigel. 'What was it again?'

'Pretty Polly.'

'Ditty Dolly?'

'Pretty Polly.'

'Witty Wally?'

'Pretty Polly.'

'Gitty Golly?'

'No! What is the matter with you?' said Alan, stamping his foot.

'I'm a bit hard of hearing. All those cannons, you know, they've played havoc with my ears.'

'You don't have ears.'

'Well that doesn't help either,' agreed Nigel.

'All right. Forget about the parroting. Just stand on my shoulder,' said Alan.

'Oh I can't do that,' said Nigel. 'Health and safety. I might fall.'

'You're a bird! You can fly!'

'Nevertheless, I will need a harness or it will break several health and safety rules. And then you could lose your licence. And be struck off.'

'This is ridiculous!' fumed Alan.

'I don't make the rules,' said Nigel.

Alan turned and kicked a bucket angrily.

Hang on, he kicked a bucket. The bucket! There's the bucket we've been looking for! It was under Alan's hammock all along.

'Rurret and raaade!' said Dot tearfully. Wilf quickly covered her mouth.

'What?' said Alan to Nigel.

'I didn't say anything,' said Nigel.

Alan tutted and climbed up the ladder to the deck.

Wilf and Dot crawled across the floor to the hammock. Wilf grabbed the bucket and Dot seized the spade and chewed on it happily.

Then Wilf and Dot tiptoed up the ladder. They peeped out and saw Alan trying to tie his eyepatch on. They edged slowly towards the gangplank, as silent as a smudge.

Suddenly . . .

'Hoist the anchor and set sail!' shouted Captain Alan.

And with a lurch, the pirate ship launched out to sea.

Oh no!

They were stuck!

They were trapped!

They were stowaways!

They scrunched up as small as possible and hid behind a barrel of grog.

'Right, me hearties!' said Alan.

'Yes?' said two voices in unison.

'What?' said Alan, confused.

'We're Mr and Mrs Heartie,' said a couple in matching teddy-bear jumpers.

'Not just you, not just you,' said Alan. 'I'm talking to everyone.'

'Oh sorry,' said a voice. 'I wasn't listening.'

'What?' said Alan, even more confused.

'I'm Dave Everyone,' said Dave Everyone.

'Not you – I meant *everyone*. All the pirates!' said Alan.

'They're not here. They're all asleep downstairs in their hammocks,' explained Dave Everyone.

'Fine,' said Alan. 'Just you three then. I have found this old and ancient map. And X marks the spot where the treasure is buried.'

'That sounds lovely, but we really just came for the napkin-folding lesson,' said Mr and Mrs Heartie.

'This is a pirate ship, not a cruise ship!' said Alan angrily.

'Oh dear,' said Mr Heartie. 'So no jazz night?'

'No!' said Alan.

'No songs made famous by Frank Sinatra night?' asked Mrs Heartie.

'Definitely not!' said Alan.

'No fancy dress night?' asked Mr Heartie.

'Yes there's definitely fancy dress because I've seen a lot of people dressed as pirates,' said Mrs Heartie.

'THAT'S BECAUSE THEY ARE PIRATES!'

yelled Alan in a very high-pitched voice. 'Now we are going to this remote undiscovered island – and at my command, unleash hell!' he boomed.

'The thing is,' said Dave Everyone, 'I'd love to unleash hell but I'm feeling a little bit seasick. Can I unleash hell tomorrow?'

'I suppose so,' said Alan. 'What about you two?'

'We want our money back,' said Mr and Mrs Heartie.

'Fine. I'll unleash hell on my own,' said Alan sadly. 'As usual.'

'You could always take the stowaways,' said Mrs Heartie.

'Who?' said Alan.

'Those two, crouching behind the barrel there,' said Mrs Heartie, pointing towards Wilf and Dot.

Wilf felt his hair go all hot. Then his ears went all buzzy and his knees tried to go the wrong way.

'Oh we've got stowaways, have we?' roared
Alan.

'No, it's just me and Dot and we're only
here by accident,' said Wilf in a trembly voice,
'because Dot wanted her—'

'Rurret and raaaade!' wailed Dot.

'Do you know what pirates do with stowaways?' said Alan.

'No,' said Wilf anxiously.

'Neither do I,' said Alan. 'I haven't got that far in the **"How to Be a Pirate"** manual – but I expect it's not very nice.'

'No, you're probably right,' agreed Wilf.

'In the meantime, you can help me get the buried treasure,' he said. 'Follow me!'

And with that he scampered up the rigging.

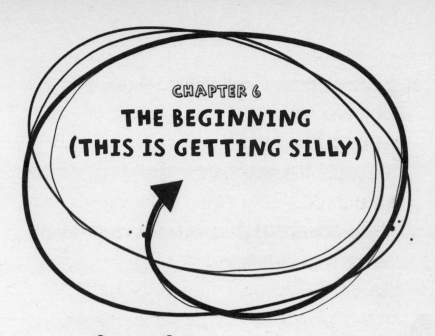

CHAPTER 6
THE BEGINNING
(THIS IS GETTING SILLY)

'Land **ahargh!**' shouted Alan because the pirate ship hit a remote undiscovered island and he fell off the rigging and bumped his nose on the deck.

'Land **ahargh!** Land **ahargh!**' repeated Nigel.

'No don't repeat that!' said Alan. 'I said it wrong.'

'Land **ahargh!**' said Nigel.

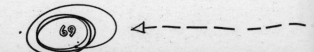

'I meant to say land ahoy!' explained Alan. 'But then I fell over.'

'Land **ahargh!**' said Nigel.

'Because the ship hit the island,' continued Alan.

'Land **ahargh!**' said Nigel, more loudly.

'Stop!' shouted Alan.

'Shop!' said Nigel.

'Ooh I like a nice shop,' said Mr Heartie.

'Does it have knick-knacks?' said Mrs Heartie.

'**Shut up!**' said Alan. 'I, Long John Alan—'

'**Shut up!**' said Nigel.

'I, Long John Alan, am going to claim this island—' persevered Alan.

'**Shut up!**' said Nigel.

'And all the treasure on it,' said Alan, doing

his best to ignore Nigel. 'Because I am the fiercest pirate in the whole world and *everyone—*'

'Did you call?' said Dave Everyone from the back of the ship.

'No I didn't. I'm in the middle of a speech if you don't mind—'

'Shut up!' said Nigel.

'And everyone fears and respects me.'

'Shut up!' repeated Nigel.

'I don't fear and respect you,' said Dave Everyone, coming over, 'but I don't really know you. Maybe I will when I get to know you.'

Alan closed his eyes and massaged his temples for a few moments.

'Right, come on, stowaways, let's lower the gangplank.'

Wilf helped Alan lower the gangplank and

watched while Alan marched on to the beach
of the remote undiscovered island.

'And I shall name this land . . .' said Alan
grandly, **'Alan Land.'** And he stuck
a flag in the beach. Then he thought for a
second and pulled the flag out again. 'Or is
Aland better?' he asked.

'I prefer the Isle of Wight. Which is where you are,' said an old lady who was walking her dog.

'Nonsense,' said Alan crossly. 'This is an undiscovered island which I have just discovered. And I shall call it the United States of Alan.'

He planted his flag back in the beach again.

The old lady's dog immediately did a wee on Alan's flagpole.

'Treason!' shouted Alan. 'Lock him up for treason.'

'Come on, Trevor, don't wee on the flagpole,' said the old lady to her dog.

Trevor trotted over to Kevin Phillips and sniffed his bottom and then Kevin Phillips sniffed Trevor's bottom.

'Why has your dog got a cone round its neck?' asked the old lady.

'He is not a dog,' explained Alan. 'His name is Kevin Phillips and he is my right-hand man.'

'And why has he got a cone round his neck?' repeated the old lady.

'Because he keeps biting his bottom,' said Alan reluctantly.

'Yes, mine does that. Stupid animals,' said the old lady cheerily.

'I can't hear you because you're not here and you don't exist,' said Alan. 'I am the first person to set foot on these shores and

I am now going to salute my flag and sing my national anthem to myself.' And then he started singing, in a very high voice:

'**God save my gracious Alan,**

Long live my noble Alan,

God save the Alan ...'

'That is a dreadful racket,' complained the old lady. 'May I suggest that you remove your flag and yourself from this beach or I will have to call the police.'

'Listen,' said Alan, 'there is a long tradition of brave explorers like me discovering new countries and then finding there are very annoying people already living there who have beaten them to it.'

'Yes,' said the old lady. 'So the best thing for you to do is take your flag and go home.'

'No,' said Alan, 'the best thing for me to do

is kill you all and then pretend you weren't here. You are nothing more than savages.'

Alan marched back to his ship. 'Come on, stowaways. And welcome to the **United States of Great Alan Land,**' he said.

'It's the Isle of Wight,' said the old lady in the background.

'Ignore the savages,' said Alan to Wilf and Dot. 'Now, looking at this map, the treasure must be in that cave over there. And your job is to go and get it.'

'The thing is,' said Wilf, 'I'm scared of caves because I worry there might be bears living in them. And I'm scared of bears.'

'Oh there won't be a bear,' said Alan.

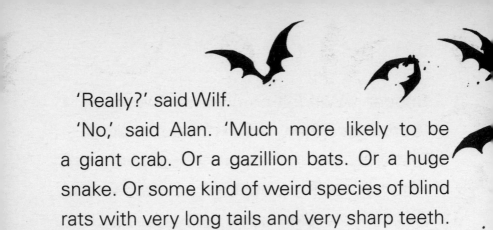

'Really?' said Wilf.

'No,' said Alan. 'Much more likely to be a giant crab. Or a gazillion bats. Or a huge snake. Or some kind of weird species of blind rats with very long tails and very sharp teeth. Or maybe a nest of scorpions.'

Suddenly Wilf felt much, much worse.

'Come on then, off you go,' said Alan impatiently.

'OK,' said Wilf, 'I just need to do something.'

And he delved in his backpack for his 'How to Stop Worrying' leaflet.

Number four said **'Distract yourself by doing something else, like dancing.'** Wilf hated dancing, but anything was worth a try.

He started doing a slow sort of shy sort of shuffly dance. Dot and Alan and Mr and Mrs Heartie and Dave Everyone and the old lady from the beach (and her dog) all stared at him.

Wilf could feel himself blushing. This wasn't helping at all. Maybe he needed to do a faster, sproingier kind of dance.

He tried lifting his knees and throwing his arms out and he did a few jumps.

Dot and Alan and Mr and Mrs Heartie
and Dave Everyone and the old lady from
the beach (and her dog) continued to stare,
looking utterly bemused.

Maybe the leaflet meant a more traditional
sort of dance. Wilf started doing a more
marchy swoopy spinny sort of dance with a
very serious expression on his face.

Dot and Alan and Mr and Mrs Heartie and Dave Everyone and the old lady from the beach (and her dog) all took a step backward, looking extremely perplexed. Mr and Mrs Heartie told Alan that if this was the entertainment they wanted their money back. Again.

Wilf was mortified. He would much rather be in a dark cave with bears and crabs than have to dance while people stared at him, so he picked up his backpack and ran into the cave. It was as cold and damp in there as an old teabag.

Wilf got a torch from his backpack so that he could see if there was a bear or a big crab or anything else scuttly or nibbly or stingy. And he had some packed lunch which he could throw if the bear or the crab or the nibbly scuttly thing looked hungry. And he also had his slippers because he took his slippers everywhere because they were comfy and comforting, but also he could run super-fast in his slippers – faster than a bear or a crab or a nibbly scuttly thing.

Wilf tiptoed slowly to the back of the cave, in his slippers. Suddenly, he heard a sort of raspy sound.

What was that?

Shh!

There it was again!

He tried to think what animal might make a raspy sound. A bear with a cough? A crab with an allergy? No, it was just Wilf doing panicky breathing. He tried to panic more quietly and continued on his way.

Suddenly, he heard a sort of squelchy sound.

What was that?

Shh!

There it was again!

He tried to think what might squelch. A scorpion with a cold? A bat chewing on chewing gum?

No, it was just his slippers squeaking as he walked.

He tried to walk more quietly and continued on his way.

Suddenly he heard a sort of whimpering sound.

What was that?

Shh!

There it was again!

It sounded like a small boy whimpering

with fear. Maybe Wilf was whimpering with fear. But no, it wasn't him. He whimpered and his whimper was a different kind of whimper altogether.

He peered through the darkness. At the back of the cave he could see something. Look – there! No, not there – over there! Left a bit, down a bit, right a bit – the treasure chest!

And something else, next to the treasure chest – a dark shadow. Wilf shone his torch at it. It was a small whimpering boy.

'Please don't hurt me!' said the boy.

'Who are you?' said Wilf.

'I'm Jack and I'm scared there might be a bear in this cave.'

'There are no bears,' said Wilf. 'And no crabs, bats, rats, snakes or scorpions either.'

Jack gulped loudly.

'But I heard a sort of raspy sound and then a squelchy sound,' said Jack anxiously.

'Yes that was me,' said Wilf.

'And then a sort of farting sound,' added Jack.

'Yes we don't need to mention that. Anyway, what are you doing here?' Wilf asked, changing the subject.

'I found this treasure,' said Jack. 'And I'm keeping it.'

'Oh dear,' said Wilf. 'I was rather hoping to have it.'

'No it's mine and I'm keeping it forever and ever,' said Jack. 'Unless . . .' he added, looking Wilf up and down, 'you want to do swapsies?'

'Yes!' said Wilf. 'What would you like?'

'Is that a picnic you're holding?' asked Jack hungrily.

'Yes, yes it is,' said Wilf.

'I'll have the biscuits and the torch and your slippers,' said Jack.

'Yes, all right, deal!'

The two boys shook hands and Wilf picked up the treasure chest and made his way out of the cave again.

'Yes! Yes! You did it!' crowed Alan when he saw Wilf holding the treasure chest. 'Now I'm going to be the richest pirate in the whole world and I'm going to buy a new

Big Gun Thingy

and then people will fear and respect me and I will be the baddest, the baddest, the biddly boddly baddest man in the whole wide— Oh poo.'

Alan stopped mid-boast when he opened the treasure chest and saw what was inside.

It wasn't diamonds and pearls and emeralds and rubies and other glinty gleamy shiny things. It was some old copies of a pirate comic book, some interestingly shaped pebbles, a goldfish bowl with a plastic fish in it, some (mouldy) sweets, a rubber ring, a fishing rod and a cricket bat.

'That's not treasure!' shouted Alan crossly.

'Well it is if you like pebbles and comics,' said Wilf. 'Which I do!'

'It's worthless!' said Alan.

'Now hang on,' said Wilf. 'I spent two slippers on this. And a torch and some biscuits. So you see, it's not worthless.'

'Well you can have it then,' said Alan. 'I'm going to get myself some *proper* treasure by robbing other ships like a *proper* pirate.'

And *that's* when the

whole kerfuffle

started. NO BUT IT REALLY, REALLY, REALLY IS THIS TIME!

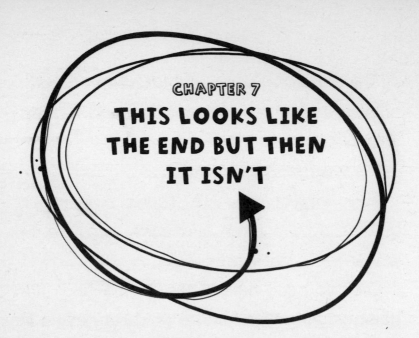

CHAPTER 7

THIS LOOKS LIKE THE END BUT THEN IT ISN'T

Alan marched his stowaways back to his pirate ship. Wilf felt as sad as a single sock. He was homesick, he had lost his best slippers and he was as sorry as a peanut that he had ever come on board Alan's ship. At least Dot was happy, still chewing on her spade and hitting her bucket against her head cheerily.

But Wilf wasn't happy. He was pining for Stuart. Stuart would have known how to make him feel better. Stuart would have cheered him up.

Wilf could feel that he was about to cry so he tried to whistle. But it's very difficult to make your mouth go in an **'o'** shape when it wants to go in a **'waaaaaaaah'** shape.

He managed a few notes but they were rather wobbly and forlorn. He hated being a stowaway. He wished he were at home.

Then out of the corner of his eye he noticed something. Someone waving. Some*thing* waving. With all fourteen arms. Could it be? It couldn't be! It was!

Stuart had crawled out of Wilf's top pocket! Stuart had stowed away on Wilf!

'Oh, Stuart! I'm so pleased to see you!' gasped Wilf. 'But you are a very naughty woodlouse,' he added, trying to look frowny and stern. 'But I'm so glad you're a naughty woodlouse because if you weren't you wouldn't be here!'

Wilf kissed Stuart.

Stuart nuzzled into Wilf. They did their secret handshake (fourteen times) and Wilf showed Stuart his treasure. He began to feel much, much better. Until . . .

'**Ahoy, me hearties, brace the main sail, hoist the Jolly Roger, avast the something or others, fire the cannons!**' shouted Alan.

'Sorry,' said Mr and Mrs Heartie. 'We're too busy watching *The Phantom of the Opera* in the theatre. Scurvy Steve has organized a special showing.'

'What about everyone else?' asked Alan.

'It's not a good time right now,' said Dave Everyone, 'cos we're playing bingo and Cut-throat Cuthbert says you can win a hamper.'

'What about the stowaways?' asked Alan.

'It's just that Tommy the Toothless said he'd teach us how to fold napkins into the shape of a swan,' said Wilf.

'But we're pirates,' said Alan, 'and I've spotted another ship in the distance – we've got to get those landlubbers, pillage their grog and booty, put it on the poop deck and shiver me timbers.'

Some of the pirates danced past, doing the conga.

Alan turned to Nigel. 'Say something.'

'Hmm?' said Nigel. 'Like what?'

Alan sighed. 'You know, you know – brace the main sail, grog, booty, shiver me timbers – all that stuff,' said Alan impatiently.

'Lace the chain mail?' asked Nigel.

'Brace the main sail.'

'Chase the main whale?' asked Nigel.

'Brace the main sail,' repeated Alan.

'Race the plane tail?' asked Nigel.

Before Alan could say a very naughty swear word, they caught up with the ship because it turned out that Alan had been

looking through his telescope the wrong way,
so in fact it wasn't

a tiny ship, far away,

it was an

ENORMOUS AIRCRAFT CARRIER VERY CLOSE UP!

'**Yikes,**' said Alan. '**Fire the cannons!**'

'Hire the salmons?' said Nigel.

'Sink the ship!' commanded Alan.

'Shrink the chip?' said Nigel.

'Shoot the parrot!' said Alan, jumping up and down with rage.

'Toot the carrot?' said Nigel, perplexed. 'It would be easier to repeat everything you said if you ever said anything that made any sense,' he complained.

'Drat!' shouted Alan indignantly.

'Sprat?' said Nigel. 'Don't mind if I do. I'm a bit partial to fish. Although I can't do shellfish,' he added. 'I have an intolerance.'

Alan sighed and went over to one of the cannons and lit it.

There was a fizzing. And then a pause. And then an enormous . . .

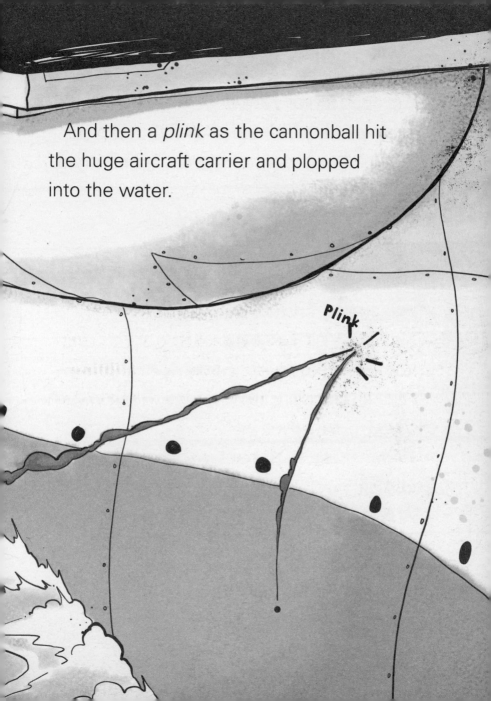

And then a *plink* as the cannonball hit the huge aircraft carrier and plopped into the water.

Plink

Alan fired all the cannons.

Plink plink plink plink plink.

They hit the aircraft carrier and plopped one by one into the water.

Alan turned and looked at Wilf.

'Did you just laugh?' said Alan.

'No,' said Wilf.

'You smiled though,' said Alan.

'No,' said Wilf truthfully.

'Your eyes are smiling,' said Alan.

'I think I just have smiley eyes. They do it on their own,' explained Wilf.

'Right. That's it. You are walking the plank!' said Alan.

WHAT?? Walking the plank??

Wilf's eyeballs went all hot and swivelly, he gulped a big gulp and his knees tried to go the wrong way.

If he walked the plank he would fall in the water and he hated falling in water and getting his face wet. And he was scared a big squashy squid would eat him up in a very squishy way.

What was he going to do? He wanted to knit the word 'HELP' and hang it from the mast.

But he didn't have time for knitting. And he didn't have needles for knitting. And he didn't have wool for knitting. Knitting was out of the question. So instead he had a great big old worry and then a great big think and he thought so hard his brain got a stitch. And then he had an idea.

He got out his 'How to Stop Worrying' leaflet. Number five said 'Break down the thing you are worried about into little steps.'

Right. So. He had to take one step along

the plank, then another step along the plank, then another step along the plank, then another step along the plank, then another step along the plank, then another step along the plank, then another step along the plank – this wasn't really helping much – then he had to **faaaaaalllll**, and **faaaaaallll** some more, keep **faaaaaaaallllling**, keep **faaaaaaallllling**, keep **faaaaaaaallllling** – it was not helping at all – down into the water right into the flobberdy slobberdy jaws of a squishy squid who would suck him up, **squelch squeeeelchhhhhhhh . . .**

STOP! Thinking about it was making him feel much worse. Best to just get on with it.

Wilf kissed Stuart goodbye and popped him into Dot's bucket. Then he took the goldfish bowl from the treasure chest which he popped on to his head (so he wouldn't get his face wet). He also got from his backpack a tin of sardines (from the picnic) to offer to the squishy squid to eat instead of himself and a tin opener to help the squishy squid open the sardines.

And with that, Wilf plunged into the water and floated . . .

down

down

down

down

down

down

down

down

down

down

until . . .

THWUMP!

He landed on something hard. Not a squashy squid. Maybe a squid wearing a hard hat?

Wilf listened out for any squelchy squiddy noises.

He heard a muffled shout.

'Oi, get off my submarine!' the muffled shout said.

Then suddenly Wilf felt himself going . . .

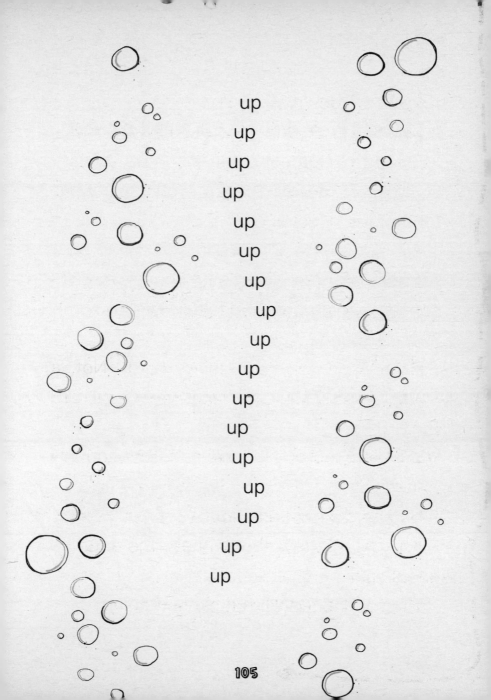

up
up
up
up
up
up
up
up
up
up
up
up
up
up
up
up

until . . .

splash-cough-phatooee.

He had plunged into the air. In an upward plungy sort of way. There's probably a word for that.

Wilf sat up. He appeared to be sitting on a submarine. There were some squeaky creaky sounds coming from inside followed by some sweary sounds.

'Dash it all to hell. The damned hatch has stuck closed. Damn and blast it,' said the voice. 'Do you think you could help open it up?' it asked.

'Well, I'll have a go,' said Wilf. He got out his tin opener and very carefully went round the whole of the top of the round hatch of the submarine and flipped it open.

As it opened, a very cross face with a big moustache emerged.

'What do you think you're doing, you blithering nincompoop?' said the cross face.

'Well I was dying and you interrupted me,' explained Wilf.

'Well don't die all over my submarine, I've just had it washed.' said the cross face.

'Who are you?' asked Wilf.

'Captain Bailey at your service. All present and correct.' He saluted and poked himself in the eye. 'Ouch. Dash it. Never have got the hang of that.'

Wilf saluted back.

'Well come in if you're coming in. Don't want you-know-who seeing,' said Captain Bailey.

Wilf climbed into the submarine and Captain Bailey closed the hatch and the submarine dived under the water in a very creaky drippy groany way.

'What are you doing down here?' said Wilf.

'Been down here for seventy-five years. Not seen much action for quite some time, but I'm ready for 'em. Crafty bunch they are.'

'Who?' asked Wilf.

'It's probably best if we speak in code. In case they're listening,' said Captain Bailey, and he tapped his nose twice.

'Was that the code?' asked Wilf. 'The nose-tapping?'

'No, no, that was just – you know – a nod and a wink.'

'The code is nodding and winking?' asked Wilf.

'Dash it all to hell, boy, no! Pay attention. Right. So instead of saying "war", we'll say **"tiddlywinks"**. Got it?'

'Yes, sir,' said Wilf.

'And instead of saying "Germans", we'll say **"chinchillas".**'

'Righty ho,' said Wilf.

'So the English are playing **tiddlywinks** with the **chinchillas** and – hang on a minute,' said Captain Bailey. 'You're not one of them are you? You're not . . .' his eyes widened in horror, '**a chinchilla?**'

'No, sir,' said Wilf.

'Ah, but that's what you would say. If you were a **chinchilla** in disguise. Wouldn't put it past them, hairy little blighters.'

Wilf was getting a little bit confused.

'I promise I'm not a **chinchilla,**' said Wilf. 'But even if I was a **chinchilla**, the English aren't playing **tiddlywinks** with the **chinchillas** any more.'

'Balderdash!' said Captain Bailey. And then, 'Excuse my French.'

'No, no, I promise. They haven't played **tiddlywinks** for years,' said Wilf.

'What?' said Captain Bailey in a high-pitched shriek. 'Did the **chinchillas** win? Did they take Poland and then take over the world?'

'No,' said Wilf. 'It's all fine. It's over. We're all friends. In fact, my cousin is a German, I mean a **chinchilla**.'

Captain Bailey sat down and had a very long think.

'Well crikey o' blimey, I don't know what to say,' said Captain Bailey. 'And I don't know what to do,' he added sadly. 'This game of **tiddlywinks** has been my life. I don't know how to do anything else.'

Captain Bailey began to cry and then began

to blow his nose in a loud trumpety way. 'You know, one Christmas, me and the **chinchillas**, we put our **tiddlywinks** aside and we had a jolly good game of, well, in actual fact, it was tiddlywinks.'

'Please don't be sad,' said Wilf.

Then an idea began to form in Wilf's mind.

'Because there's something much worse than a **chinchilla** to deal with now,' said Wilf.

Captain Bailey looked up, mid-trumpet.

'Oh yes,' said Wilf. 'And this time, it's bigger than **tiddlywinks**.'

'What do you mean, boy? Come on, spit it

out!' said Captain Bailey excitedly.

'Well, Alan . . .' started Wilf.

'In code, in code!'

'Sorry. There's this man called . . .'

'**Delilah?**' offered Captain Bailey.

'If you like. And he wants to . . . **crochet a tea cosy**,' said Wilf, giving a meaningful wink.

Captain Bailey gasped. 'No!' he said. 'He wouldn't!'

'I'm afraid he would, sir,' said Wilf.

'That's dreadful!' said Captain Bailey.

'I know!'

'He must be stopped!'

'Yes, sir!'

'Just so I know,' said Captain Bailey, 'what are we actually talking about?'

'He wants to destroy the world,' explained Wilf.

'Oh he does, does he?' bellowed Captain Bailey furiously. 'Well he hasn't counted on Captain Bailey and . . . and . . . what's your name, boy?'

'Wilf,' said Wilf.

'Wilf is it?' said Captain Bailey. 'Then I shall call you . . .' Captain Bailey scratched his chin, trying to think of a good name.

'How about Wilf?' suggested Wilf.

'Could I? It would be so much easier,' said Captain Bailey with relief.

'Come on, Captain Bailey!' urged Wilf. 'After that pirate ship!'

CHAPTER 8
I'LL BE HONEST, THINGS AREN'T LOOKING GOOD FOR WILF

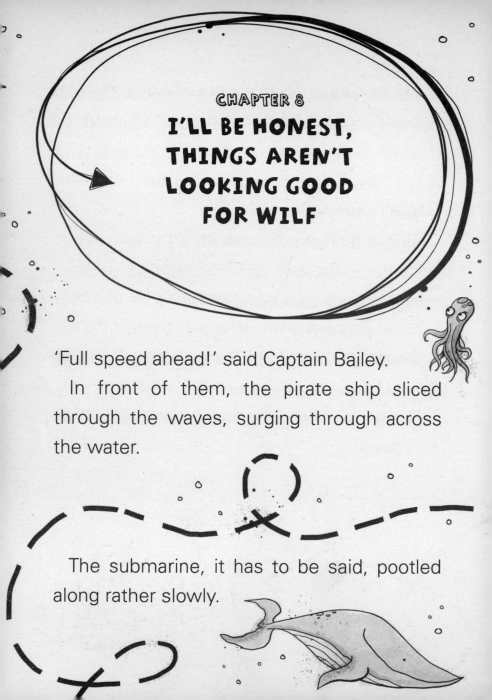

'Full speed ahead!' said Captain Bailey.

In front of them, the pirate ship sliced through the waves, surging through across the water.

The submarine, it has to be said, pootled along rather slowly.

'You know that thing you said about full speed?' asked Wilf tentatively. 'Could we do it?'

'This is it, lad, hold on to your hat!' said Captain Bailey excitedly.

Surge surge went the pirate ship.

Pootle pootle went the submarine.

Surgey surge surge went the pirate ship.

Pootley pootle pootle went the submarine.

Surgety surgety surge surge surge went the pirate ship.

Pootley pootley poot poot poot went the submarine.

'We need to hurry, otherwise **Delilah** will have **crocheted** that **tea cosy** before we even get there,' said Wilf anxiously. 'And also, my sister and my best friend are on there and we have to get them back!' Wilf's voice went all wobbly and he had to go and look at a notice about escape procedures as though he was very interested in it.

'Don't worry. The pirate ship seems to be going in circles,' said Captain Bailey. 'Periscope up!' he barked.

And then he turned another squeaky handle.

Wilf peeped through the periscope. Captain Bailey was right! The pirate ship *was* going in circles. And they were catching up with it!

Wilf could see Alan and Dave Everyone fighting over the wheel of the pirate ship. Nearby, Eyepatch Eddie was teaching Mr and

Mrs Heartie how to fold napkins into swans.

'Pirate ship at eleven o'clock!' said Wilf excitedly.

'Oh I think we're going to get there much more quickly than that,' said Captain Bailey.

CLAAAAAAAANNNNNNNNNGGGG went the submarine as it hit the pirate ship.

'See what I mean?' said Captain Bailey.

Wilf and Captain Bailey climbed aboard the pirate ship, as nimbly and as silently as a couple of very large nimble silent squirrels. The first thing Wilf saw was Dot, chewing her spade happily.

'I'm so pleased to see you!' said Wilf to Dot, kissing her and leaving a little clean patch on her cheek.

'And I'm so happy to see you too, Stuart!' said Wilf, kissing Stuart.

Wilf stopped to look at Stuart.

'You are looking very handsome today,' said Wilf. 'Have you polished your segments? Have you combed your antennae? What's going on?'

Stuart blushed. Then he giggled. Then he gave a big smile. And then a tiny woodworm crawled out of a hole on the ship, crawled over to Stuart and shyly held one of Stuart's hands.

'Have you had a holiday romance?' asked Wilf.

Stuart nodded.

'With this beautiful woodworm?'

Stuart and Wendy (the woodworm) giggled and blushed.

'Well I am so happy for you both,' said Wilf.

'SEIZE HIM!' yelled Alan, spotting Wilf.

'*Cheese* him?' asked Nigel.

'Seize,' repeated Alan.

'*Squeeze?*' asked Nigel.

'Seize,' said Alan loudly.

'*Sneeze?*' said Nigel.

'Is anybody around here going to **seize** that boy?' asked Alan.

'We're just a bit busy with our napkin swans at the moment,' said Mr and Mrs Heartie.

'And I'm learning how to ballroom dance,' said Dave Everyone.

'Pirates?' asked Alan.

'Oh now go, walk out the door, just turn around now . . .' sang the pirates, because they were doing karaoke.

JUST TURN
AROUND NOW,
♪

'While we're waiting for someone to seize me,' said Wilf, 'I'd like to introduce you to my new friend, Captain Bailey. Captain Bailey, this is Alan.'

'**Delilah**. Delighted to meet you. I've heard a lot about you,' said Captain Bailey.

Alan looked baffled.

'Captain Bailey saved my life,' explained Wilf.

'Typical!' said Alan. 'But it's probably a good thing you're back because I have a new plan.'

'Is it to put all our differences aside and have a jolly good game of tiddlywinks?' asked Captain Bailey. 'By which I mean actual tiddlywinks, not **tiddlywinks**,' he explained.

'No. It is an evil plan to get the biggest cannon in the world and then fire it at the world and sink it. Because I am the baddest, the baddest, the biddly boddly baddest man in the whole wide worlderoony,' said Alan proudly.

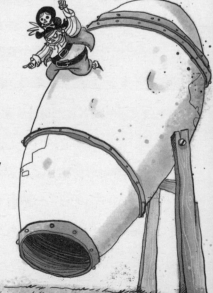

'But dash it all to hell, Delilah, where are you going to get the biggest cannon in the world?' asked Captain Bailey.

'I'm not sure. What I really need is a huge long metal cylinder-shaped thingy. Something like . . .' Alan looked around for inspiration.

Then his eyes fell on the submarine.

'Your submarine!' he said.

'**No!**' cried Captain Bailey.

'**Yes!**' cried Alan.

'You wouldn't!' cried Captain Bailey.

'I would!' cried Alan.

'You couldn't!' cried Captain Bailey.

'I could!' cried Alan.

'You shouldn't!' cried Captain Bailey.

'I should!' cried Alan.

'You must!' cried Captain Bailey.

'I mustn't!' cried Alan.

'You will!' cried Captain Bailey.

'No I won't!' cried Alan. 'Oh, hang on. Wait a minute. Back up. We've swapped roles.'

'We haven't!' cried Captain Bailey.

'Yes we have!' cried Alan. 'You're saying I must and I'm saying I mustn't.'

'My dear chap, you're quite right. I'm so sorry,' said Captain Bailey. 'Shall we start again?'

'I haven't really got time,' said Alan. 'I've got rather a lot on, what with sawing the ends of your submarine off.'

'Yes. Fair point,' said
Captain Bailey.

CHAPTER 9

EEK, NOW IT'S ALL GOT WORSE

Well, I don't know how often you've tried to saw the ends off a submarine, but it is jolly hard work. Unless, of course, you happen to have a robot to hand.

'LRX2FL309version8.4markIII!' called Alan.

'LRX2FL309version8.4markIII!' called Alan again.

'**Mark III!**' screamed Alan.

The robot galumphed on to deck. 'What?' he said.

'I need you to do something for me,' said Alan.

'I can't. I don't feel well,' said Mark III.

'What's wrong?' asked Alan, concerned.

'I'm tired,' said Mark III.

'You've been asleep for three weeks!' exclaimed Alan, a little exasperated.

'And I feel sick,' added Mark III.

Alan put a hand against Mark III's shiny head.

'You do feel hot,' admitted Alan.

'See? I'm not well!' whined Mark III.

'Hang on a minute. I can smell oil on your breath. Have you been drinking oil?' said Alan.

'No. Maybe. Wh-what if I have?' stammered Mark III.

'I told you not to drink too much oil! It's not good for you!' said Alan.

'But all my friends do it and anyway I didn't drink much and anyway you can't tell me what to do!' said Mark III.

'Yes I can,' said Alan, 'because I invented you and I built you and I programmed you to do my every bidding and so now, if you don't mind, I would like you to saw the ends off that—'

'I'm going to be sick!' wailed Mark III before Alan could finish his sentence and he clattered off down the steps back to his hammock.

Alan sighed.

'I just want someone to saw the end off a submarine!' he said dejectedly. 'Is that *so* much to ask?'

'Is it a cruise ship game?' asked Mrs Heartie.

'**No!**' snapped Alan.

'Are there teams?' asked Mr Heartie.

'**No!**' snapped Alan.

'Is there a prize?' asked Mrs Heartie.

'**No!**' snapped Alan. 'I mean yes. Yes there is a prize. The prize is . . . the prize is . . . the prize is . . . a hamper,' he said, pleased with himself.

'Ooh, a hamper!' said Mr and Mrs Heartie and they both rushed off to each saw an end off the submarine.

And a mere eighteen hours later, Mrs Heartie had won and had claimed the 'hamper', which was actually the rest of Wilf's picnic.

'So what happens now?' asked Wilf anxiously.

'Simple. We find a volcano, melt a whole heap of metal and build the world's biggest cannonball. It's obvious isn't it?' said Alan.

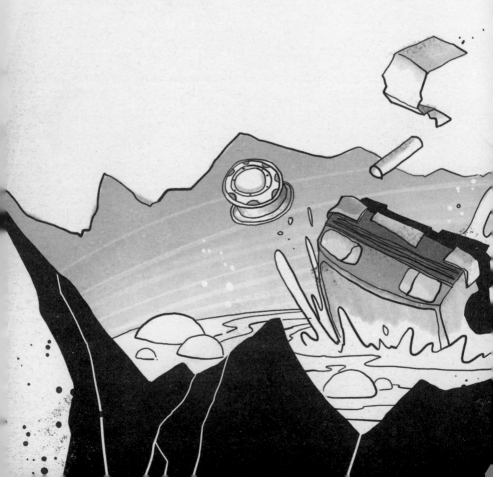

'Not that obvious, no,' said Wilf.

'Right. Question,' said Alan. 'Where is there a volcano?'

'Ooh, is it quiz night?' asked Mr Heartie.

'Is there a prize?' asked Mrs Heartie.

'I'm not so good at geography questions – can you do more eighties pop?' said Mr Heartie.

'I just need to know where a volcano is,' said Alan impatiently.

'I've got a better one,' said Dave Everyone. 'Who sang "West End Girls"?'

'Ooh, ooh, I know,' said Mr Heartie. 'Was it Pet Shop Boys?'

'Correct! And for a bonus point,' continued Dave Everyone, 'what was the name of— '

'Can we just FOCUS!' shouted Alan. 'I need to know where there is a volcano! Now!'

Nobody answered.

'Come on! You must know!' Alan insisted.

'All right, all right. There's a cash prize,' sighed Alan, relenting.

'Hawaii!' said Mrs Heartie.

'Ooh very good,' said Mr Heartie.

'Do I win? How much do I win?' asked Mrs Heartie excitedly.

Alan fished around in his pockets.

'Two pounds and seventy-three pence, a button, a squashed toffee and a bit of fluff.'

'Whoopeee!' said Mrs Heartie.

'It's an expensive business being a pirate,' complained Alan. 'Right, which way is Hawaii?'

'I know,' squawked Nigel. 'Because I've flown all over the world. I'm like your own personal satnav.'

'Perfect!' said Alan.

'Then take us to Hawaii please!'

'No problem,' said Nigel. 'I know a really good shortcut.'

CHAPTER 10
NERVOUS READERS SHOULD NOT READ THIS CHAPTER

Much, much later . . .

'We've passed that bit of seaweed eighteen times!' yelled Alan, hopping from foot to foot with frustration.

'Please continue north for one hundred metres, then turn left at the next whale,' said Nigel.

'I can't turn left. There's a big bit of land in the way,' fumed Alan.

'Turn right, eight nautical miles ago,' continued Nigel.

'You stupid parrot!'

'Do a U-turn at your earliest convenience,' said Nigel.

'That's it. I'm not listening to you any more!' yelled Alan.

'You have reached your destination,' said Nigel. 'Your route guidance is now finished,' he added. And then he closed his eyes and went to sleep.

Wilf looked around him. Hawaii was not how he had imagined it would be. There were giant icebergs, frozen seas and huge snowflakes falling from the sky. Where were the blue seas and the palm trees and the coconuts?

'This isn't Hawaii!' said Alan.

Oh! That might explain it, thought Wilf.

'Where are we?' asked Alan.

Everybody tried to look busy because they weren't sure of the answer.

'You, boy!' said Alan.

'Me?' asked Wilf.

'Yes, you. Climb up to the crow's nest and see if you can spot Hawaii.'

'Why is there a crow's nest on a boat?' asked Wilf, baffled.

'It's not a real crow's nest, you nincompoop!' yelled Alan. **'It's just called a crow's nest. It's actually a lookout point used by pirates at the very, very tippity top of the tallest mast.'**

Wilf's ears went all burny. And he did three loud swallows in a row and then a strange sort of gulpy half swallow. Then his eyes went all fuzzy. One knee went the wrong way and one knee went the right way so he did a strange sort of curtsey to Alan.

'Come on. Hurry up,' said Alan.

Wilf didn't move. You see, Wilf is scared of heights. Really scared. In fact, he'd been hoping he wouldn't grow any taller because he was worried he might feel a bit fainty if he got above four feet.

What was he going to do? He wanted to run and he wanted to hide and he wanted to lie on the floor and be as low down as possible.

But he didn't have time for any of that. So instead he had a great big old worry and then a great big think and he thought so hard his brain needed a holiday. And then he had an idea.

He got out his **'How to Stop Worrying'** leaflet.

Number Six said *'It can be very calming to have a cup of camomile tea.'* Maybe Wilf should try that? Except chamomile is a flower and flowers make Wilf go sneezey and wheezey and that would not be calming. Also Wilf does NOT like tea. It makes him feel all bleurgh. And tea is very hot and Wilf is scared of scalding himself and burning his tongue. The last time Wilf tried tea it had gone down the wrong way and made Wilf choke and that had been very coughy and worrying. Worst of all, he didn't have his own cup with him so he would have to use a cup that someone else might have used first and left their slobber all over. **Urgh urgh urgh!** Wilf decided he would rather climb up to the crow's nest than have a cup of yucky old slobbered-on burny hot sneezey tea.

He went to his backpack and got out some rubber gloves because they would be grippy and that would be good for climbing the mast (he carries his rubber gloves EVERYWHERE). He also borrowed the cone from around Kevin Phillips's neck because that would stop him from looking down and seeing how high up he was. (Kevin Phillips was delighted about this because that meant his teeth could be reunited with his bottom.) Then, in case the worst came to the worst and Wilf actually died of fright, he wrote a will which said:

All my worldly goods are to be divided between Dot and Stuart.
Signed Wilf

Then he walked towards the mast and started climbing in a trembly scrambly way.

With each scrambly scramble, he scraped a knee. And he only has two knees (which I believe is the typical number) so that meant each knee had a lot of scrapes.

As he scrambled and scrabbled, he did quick little panicky gaspy breaths – and because his head was in a cone, these suddenly sounded very LOUD and ECHOEY.

Gaspy gasp, gaspy gasp, gaspy gasp, gasp.

Then he heard a different noise. Not a gaspy noise. Not a knee being scraped kind of noise. Not a rubber-glove-squeaking kind of noise. More a kind of . . . **caw**.

Caw.

There it was again! Did you hear that?

Caw.

There! What was it?

Caw.

It was getting louder.

Caw!

It sounded like a bird. Maybe a . . .

CAW CAW CAW CAW CAW CAW CAW CAW CAW CAW!

. . . crow.

'Aaaaah!' said Wilf, as he reached the top of the mast and arrived at the crow's nest.

'Caw!' said the crows.

'What is it?' shouted Alan from far below.

'You do seem to have crows up here after all!' shouted Wilf.

'What do you mean? They've made a nest in my crow's nest?' shouted Alan.

'No,' said Wilf.

Before he could say any more, one of the crows plucked the cone from Wilf's head and the other plucked the will from Wilf's hand and then shredded it.

They plonked the shredded paper into the cone and then climbed in, looking very comfy indeed.

'Actually yes,' said Wilf. 'Yes, they have made a nest.'

At that moment, Nigel flew up and landed on Wilf's head.

'Would you like me to translate?' said Nigel.

'Yes please!' said Wilf. 'Can you tell them that Alan doesn't want them in his crow's nest?'

'Of course,' said Nigel. **'ALAN DOESN'T WANT YOU IN HIS CROW'S NEST!'** he shouted.

'You just said what I said only more loudly,' Wilf pointed out.

'That's how you speak foreign languages,' explained Nigel.

'I was hoping you spoke Bird,' said Wilf, 'because you're a bird.'

'Oh I do. Yes. Absolutely. I mean I'm a bit rusty. But I'll give it a go.'

'Thank you,' said Wilf.

'Caw caw Alan caw caw no wanty you caw caw in crow's nest. Caw,' said Nigel.

The crows stared at Nigel blankly.

'I don't think they understood,' said Wilf.

'Caw caw you caw caw leavey now caw caw.'

The crows continued to stare.

'Caw caw you bye bye caw caw,' said Nigel.

The crows looked at each other and did little crowy shrugs.

'Are you definitely speaking Bird?' asked Wilf.

'Yes yes. I mean, I understand more than I can speak but—'

'Caw caw caw,' said one of the crows.

'What did she say?' asked Wilf.

'Um . . . something about a badger. Or possibly kedgeree. Or maybe a forklift truck. She's speaking awfully quickly.'

'Caw caw caw!' said the crow more urgently.

'Um, I think she wants to buy a stamp. Or rent a car. Or maybe go to a museum.'

'CAW CAW CAW!' squawked the crow.

'She's saying I'm very handsome. And clever.

And she'd like to spend more time with me—'

'CAW CAW CAW!' squawked the crow, flapping her wings angrily so that Wilf and Nigel ducked back and wobbled precariously at the top of the mast.

'Do you think that maybe she's saying she's not leaving and she wants us to go away?' asked Wilf.

'Yes it could be that,' admitted Nigel.

Wilf quickly made his way back down the mast in a slippy scrambly breathless way with Nigel wobbling around on his head.

'The thing is,' explained Wilf to Alan, 'it is actually called a crow's nest and they *are* crows so you can see where the misunderstanding might have arisen . . .'

'No. Sorry. It's not good enough. I'm going to evict them,' said Alan and he started huffing and puffing up the mast. He hadn't got more than a metre when there was a distant **'caw'** and a nearby 'splat'. Alan stopped.

'Has the crow done a poo on my head?' asked Alan in a measured voice.

'No, no,' said Wilf reassuringly. 'Well, maybe a little bit. But not so you'd notice.'

'Poo head, poo head, poo head, poo head,' sang Dot delightedly.

'Just a tiny bit,' admitted Wilf.

'Poo head, poo head, great big poo head,' continued Dot.

'Would you like a hanky?' offered Wilf.

'Yes please,' said Alan.

'I'll go and get one. They're in my backpack,' said Wilf and he trotted off to get it.

Suddenly Alan stopped and stared into the distance.

'Wait a minute! Do you see what I see?' asked Alan excitedly.

'Pooey on your he-ad, pooey on your he-ad,' sang Dot in response.

'Not that, not that,' said Alan. 'That!' He pointed into the distance. 'A volcano!'

Wilf returned with his hanky and Alan wiped his head clean.

'A volcano, a volcano! We must be in Hawaii after all!'

'Or possibly Iceland,' said Mrs Heartie. 'They have one there too. Do I get a bonus point for that?'

'No you don't. You get to watch me build the biggest cannonball in the world and then fire it and sink the world and everyone on it. **Ha ha ha ha ha ha!**' said Alan.

'I don't get it,' said Dave Everyone.

'That wasn't a joke, it was an evil laugh. For I am the baddest, the baddest, the biddly boddly baddest man in the whole wide worlderoony! And soon you will all be DESTROYED!

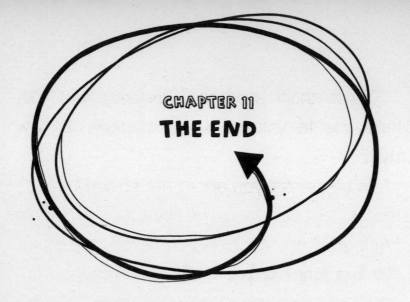

CHAPTER 11
THE END

**Oh nooooooooooooooo!
Heeeeeeeelp! We're all going to
be destroyed! Run for the hills!
I'm scared!**

I can't bear to see what happens next!

I know. I won't look. I'll just stare at this lovely flower instead. Look at the lovely flower. What a lovely flower. I do like a lovely flower.

What's that? I'm the narrator and I'm supposed to tell you what's happening? It's my job?

Can't I just tell you about the flower?

Tut.

All right.

I'll just peep between my fingers.

OK, I've peeped and I couldn't see much. Just a big metal thingy. So probably everything's fine.

What?

I have to look properly??

Gosh, it's really hard this whole being a narrator thing. The whole looking thing and the whole telling thing and the whole having to describe things all the blinking time.

All right then. I'll look properly.

Wait there . . .

Aaaaaaargh!

I've looked properly and it's hideous! Are you sure you want me to tell you? OK, if you insist. Well, while you were making me look at that stupid flower, Alan went and stole a bridge. Yes, a flipping bridge. He stole a big metal bridge because he wanted to

smush

it all up in the volcano to make the world's biggest cannonball.

'Dash it all to hell, Delilah, you can't just go around smushing bridges,' said Captain Bailey. 'You're worse than the chinchillas when they were playing tiddlywinks.'

'I have no idea what you're talking about,' said Alan.

'To be honest, neither do I any more,' admitted Captain Bailey.

'Right, me hearties,' said Alan. 'Let's drag this bridge up to that volcano. Then we can melt it and make a cannonball.'

'But Salty Sam said we were going to learn flower arranging,' said Mr and Mrs Heartie.

'Flower arranging is cancelled. Smushing bridges is this afternoon's activity.'

'Is there a—' started Mrs Heartie.

'Yes! There is a prize!' said Alan impatiently. 'The prize is . . .' He looked around for inspiration. 'Um . . . the prize is . . . Um . . . Let me think, a prize, a prize . . .'

'Did you say French fries?' said Nigel.

'A prize,' said Alan.

'Some pies?' asked Nigel.

'I need a prize,' repeated Alan.

'You have fat thighs?' asked Nigel.

'The prize is my parrot!' said Alan.

'Oh I've always wanted a parrot,' said Mrs Heartie.

'Oh I've always wanted a parrot,' parroted Nigel.

'Ha ha, he's saying what I say,' laughed Mrs Heartie.

'Ha ha, he's saying what I say,' repeated Nigel.

'That's brilliant! Let me try!' said Mr Heartie.

'That's brilliant! Let me try!' echoed Nigel.

'Hang on!' said Alan. 'So you do it for those two?'

'You threw it at goat poo?' said Nigel.

'I said you *do* it for *those two*,' repeated Alan.

'You glue it to crows' shoes?' exclaimed Nigel.

'I said you *do* it for *those two*,' repeated Alan angrily.

'You chew on some nose goo?' asked Nigel.

'**Shut up!**' screamed Alan.

'But it's hilarious!' said Mrs Heartie.

'It's hilarious!' repeated Nigel.

'Come on, let's smush the bridge! I *really* want that parrot,' said Mrs Heartie excitedly.

So Mr and Mrs Heartie and Dave Everyone and also everyone else dragged the bridge up the side of the volcano because they all wanted to win Nigel the parrot.

Now I don't know how often you've tried to stop a group of pirates dragging a bridge up a volcano in order to smush it – but no doubt you know that it isn't easy. Wilf tried to stop them, he tried to reason with them, he tried to argue with them – but they wouldn't listen. They really wanted that parrot.

Wilf stood in front of them as determined as a washing machine and he shouted,

'STOP!'

in a very serious voice with his eyebrows all frowny – but no sooner had he done so than Alan was beside him.

'Oh no you don't. We're not having any of that saving-the-world nonsense we had last time. You can keep out of it,' said Alan. 'In fact, I'm going to make sure you keep out of it, by **marooning** you.'

'But maroon would clash with my T-shirt and—'

'Not marooning you. Not painting you maroon!' shouted Alan. **'I'm going to set you adrift on an ice floe and you will be all alone at the mercy of wild animals and eventually you will sink to the bottom of**

the icy sea!' said Alan, delighted with himself. **'And then you will be dead.**

Deadity deadity dead. Deadity deadity dead dead dead,'

he added, even more delighted with himself.

'Let's go back to the whole idea of painting me maroon,' suggested Wilf.

'Nope. My mind is made up,' said Alan.

Wilf's cheeks went all burny and his ears felt all blurry and his knees tried to go the wrong way.

He didn't want to sit on an ice floe. He was scared of fish sucking his toes. And he was scared of abominable snowmen eating him. Or even ominable snowmen eating him. Actually any snowman eating him was a scary thought.

What was he going to do? He wanted to knit a big blanky and hide under it for a very long time.

But he didn't have time for knitting. And he didn't have time for hiding. So instead he had a great big old worry and then a great big think and he thought so hard his brain needed a sit-down. And then he had an idea.

Wilf went to his treasure chest and he got out the fishing rod – to catch the fish before they sucked his toes – and he got out the cricket bat, so that he could bop any snowmen on the head. Then he looked at his **'How to Stop Worrying'** leaflet. **Number five** said *It can help to make the thing you're worried about more manageable if you turn it into a song.*

'Right, put down that stupid leaflet and come with me!' barked Alan, shoving Wilf on to an ice floe and tying him up in a chain with a big padlock for good measure. As he did so, Wilf sang his song.

I don't want to sit
On a cold ice floe.
I don't want a fish
To come and suck my toe.

I don't want to be
Food for hungry fish.
I don't want my toes
To be their favourite dish.

Hey hee fiddly dee,
I worry and I fret.
Hee hee fiddly dee,
Cos I don't like getting wet.

I don't want to be
Eaten up for lunch
By a scary snowman
Going crunch crunch munch.

I don't want to be
Eaten up for tea
By a nasty snowman
Who wants to chew on me.

Hey hee fiddly dee,
I fret and I worry.
Hey hee fiddly dee,
I need help in a hurry.

But no help arrived. And Wilf was drifting further and further away.

He could see Alan, getting smaller and smaller.

He could see Dot, waving her spade, getting smaller and smaller until Dot was just a dot (with a small 'd').

Would he ever see Dot again? Would he ever see Stuart again? Would he ever see the world again? Wilf realized somebody had to do something and that someone was him and that something had to be done right

NOW.

Wilf got the fishing rod and he flicked it as hard as he could. The hook went flying towards land, flying towards Alan, flying towards Alan's belt – where the keys were hanging.

He hooked the keys and he reeled them back in. Then he unlocked the padlock and his hands were free.

Wilf grabbed the cricket bat and used it to paddle himself back to shore. He paddled and he paddled and he paddled until he felt as if his shoulder blades would catch on fire. Then as soon as he got close to land, he did a great big magnificent hop on to it. He could see the pirates nearing the top of the volcano and he scrambled up after them as fast as he could. He scrambled and he climbed and he slid and he scrambled, and he was almost at the top when suddenly he heard a loud rumbling noise.

He looked up and saw the biggest cannonball rolling down the side of the volcano towards him. It was getting bigger and bigger, it was bearing down on him . . .

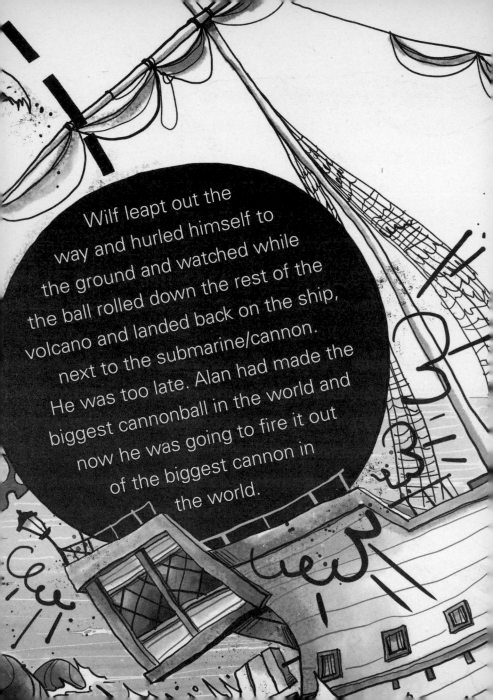

Wilf leapt out the
way and hurled himself to
the ground and watched while
the ball rolled down the rest of the
volcano and landed back on the ship,
next to the submarine/cannon.
He was too late. Alan had made the
biggest cannonball in the world and
now he was going to fire it out
of the biggest cannon in
the world.

Oh well, he'd given it his best shot, but the whole world was going to sink any second now.

Soz about that.

So this is . . .

THE END

Goodbye.

Tum ti tum.

Any minute now.

Brace yourselves.

Sinking about to commence.

So this is it.

Bye then.

Cough.

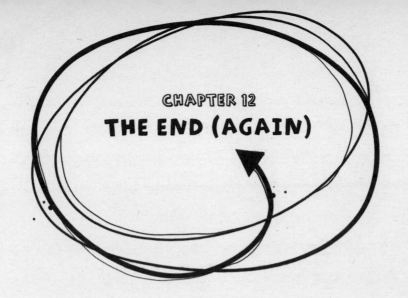

CHAPTER 12
THE END (AGAIN)

Hang on a minute. Wilf wasn't going to give up that easily.

He rushed back to the ship and went straight to his treasure chest. He got out his 'How to Stop Worrying' leaflet. But as he turned to number six, the leaflet crumbled beneath his fingers as a dozen woodworms chomped it up for their breakfast.

'Oh no!' gasped Wilf.

Then, before his very eyes, the whole treasure chest was reduced to a pile of crumbs as a couple of hundred woodworms chomped it up for *their* breakfast.

'No, no, no, no!' cried Wilf.

His leaflet was gone. His treasure was gone. Wilf was horrified. What was he going to do now? He didn't have anything to help him. He didn't have a plan. Most of all, he didn't have time to worry. And there was nothing he would have liked more than to have a big old worry. But he couldn't. It was just Wilf. Wilf against Alan. The future of the whole world depended on it. He looked over at Alan who had taken out a big box of matches and was just about to light the fuse.

Wilf rushed towards Alan and grabbed the box of matches.

He ran towards the rigging and, even though he didn't like heights, he climbed. He climbed like a monkey with its tail on fire, he climbed like a spider with its bottom on fire, he climbed and he climbed and he climbed until his arms ached and his knees screamed and his heart badoomphed in his ears.

Wilf looked down and saw Alan looking up at him. He was so far below, he looked like a tiny angry ant.

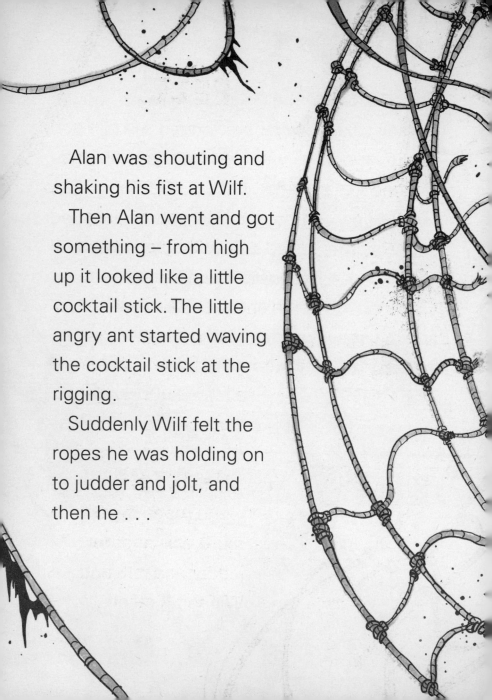

Alan was shouting and
shaking his fist at Wilf.

Then Alan went and got
something – from high
up it looked like a little
cocktail stick. The little
angry ant started waving
the cocktail stick at the
rigging.

Suddenly Wilf felt the
ropes he was holding on
to judder and jolt, and
then he . . .

FELL.

About three metres.

He was dangling
from the rigging.
He looked down
again. He could see
Alan more clearly
now. He was holding
a huge cutlass. He
took another almighty
swipe at the rigging.
SWISH!
The ropes frayed,
there was another
judder and jolt, and
Wilf felt himself . . .

FALL.

Another three or five metres.

'No!' screamed Wilf, holding on
with just one hand. 'Please stop!'

But Alan didn't stop. He took
a third huge swipe at the rigging.

SWISH!

And Wilf felt himself falling,
falling, falling until . . .

THUMP!

He fell on to
the deck, into a
pile of sawdust
– which was all
that remained of
his **'How to Stop
Worrying'** leaflet
and treasure chest.

Alan hurled himself at Wilf and tried to snatch the matches. Wilf and Alan wrestled and rolled and brawled and scrapped and tussled and scuffled and fought.

They thumped and kicked and bit and tugged and elbowed and cuffed and then finally Alan ground Wilf's face in the dust of his 'How to Stop Worrying' leaflet and he grabbed the matches.

Alan marched back over to the cannon and lit the match.

'And now,' announced Alan, **'I am going to sink the entire world, for I am the baddest, the baddest, the biddly boddly baddest man in the whole wide worlderoony.'**

And Alan lit the fuse.

Wilf watched.
Dot watched.
Stuart watched.
Wendy watched.
Captain Bailey watched.
Kevin Phillips watched.
Mark III watched.
The pirates watched.
The Hearties watched.
Dave Everyone watched.
Everyone watched.
They all held their breath.

The fuse burned lower and lower.

Wilf picked the rubber ring from the remains of his treasure chest and put it over Dot. Then he placed Stuart and Wendy on Dot's head.

The fuse burned lower and lower.

Wilf wiped the remains of his leaflet from his face.

And suddenly Wilf had an idea.

'Stuart! Ask Wendy to tell all her friends to eat the ship for breakfast. Now!'

Stuart turned and whispered something to Wendy. Then Wendy did the most enormously loud whistle. As you know, Wilf is something of an expert at whistling and this was one of the best whistles he had ever heard. No, I didn't know woodworms could whistle either, but perhaps they've just never needed to before.

Suddenly a loud munching crunching chomping noise could be heard as millions of teeny tiny mouths started chomping through the ship.

The fuse burned lower and lower.

'Goodbye world!' shouted Alan. And then he said, 'What's that strange chomping noise?'

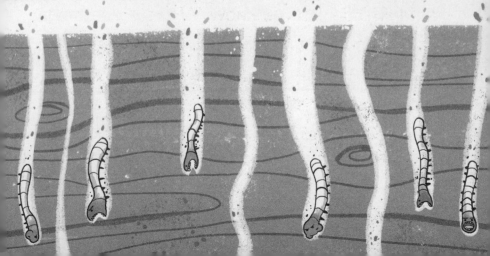

And the entire ship disappeared beneath their feet, cannon and all. And cannon and ball.

Whoosh!

Everyone splashed into the sea with a great big splash.

Pshhhhht!

The fuse of the cannon went out and the giant cannonball rolled slowly to the bottom of the ocean like a giant pebble.

'Hooray!' shouted everyone.

'I can't swimblebubblebubble!' shouted Alan.

'Bucket and spade!' said Dot, bobbing along happily in her rubber ring as she watched her beloved bucket and spade floating towards her. She grabbed the spade and chewed it happily.

Meanwhile, Kevin Phillips grabbed Alan by the collar and swam towards a nearby island.

Everyone else, including the crows, followed. Then they all climbed out of the water and on to the island and jumped up and down and hugged each other and did skippety dances.

'Hooray for Wilf and Stuart and Wendy!' shouted everyone.

'I name this island the United Alan Emirates,' said Alan, but nobody paid any attention.

'We want our money back,' said Mr and Mrs Heartie.

'You want a *funny yak*?' said Nigel.

And then Dave Everyone and *everyone* had a big picnic and they all played tiddlywinks – by which I mean tiddlywinks, not, you know, **tiddlywinks.**

And afterwards, Wilf and Dot and Stuart and Wendy went home, tired and soggy but very happy.

They didn't have the treasure nor the picnic nor the slippers and they didn't even have Wilf's precious **'How to Stop Worrying'** leaflet, but they had each other. And besides, even without his leaflet, Wilf didn't feel so worried any more.

THE END

(But it really is this time.)

Yes? Can I help?

What are you still doing here?

I said,
it's The End! Go away!

Step away
from the book . . .

Okay then. If you want to read more, you'll have to get these brilliant books!

Wilf meets Alan for the first time, and discovers his new next-door neighbour wants to destroy the world with his Big Gun Thingy!

Out now

WILF THE MIGHTY WORRIER

is KING of the JUNGLE

Coming Spring 2016

Alan tries to raise a scary Animal
Army to . . . yes, that's right . . . take
over the world! And guess
who has to stop him?

wilfthemightyworrier.com